AF614126

Bad Company.

Luke Foster

Acknowledgements

Lauren for putting up with the continual tapping of keys and also the sweet gift of the laptop that this story was written on, all my love. Mum and Dad for all your support and not forgetting Kev & Jill Beard the best in-laws a man could ask for and last but by no means least Paul and Francis, James and Angie this mention surely should be enough for a pint?

ISBN-978-1-8479956-5-0

One

I've been staring out of the same window for the last seventy-two hours with nothing but rain, clouds and smoke for company. The target is still not home, so at least someone is busy. Me? I'm waiting and watching. The blood red buses that circle below help mark the hours as I focus my attention towards the empty apartment across the street. My eyes wander from window to window in the absence of the target I'm looking for something, anything that will keep me awake and ready for action. I've been watching these apartments for so long now that even the sight of a pretty girl inspecting her slender figure in a mirror can't raise my spirits.

The hours spread out before me like an unending hourglass. The loud ticking of my cheap airport watch is a constant reminder of the time I've spent laying on the hardwood floor in this empty apartment.

The sun bleeds into the horizon and the monolithic concrete tower block opposite basks in the oranges and purples of dusk and in that moment the monstrosity of lazy architecture becomes a beautiful beacon of colour.

The street below has started to fill with Friday night revellers ready for their usual alcoholic onslaught. The neon food joints are now all open for business, the smell of chicken and grease is thick in the air, but despite the stench I keep the window open. The civilians in the bars below get louder and more obnoxious as the drink flows, thoughts of leaving this assignment and joining their ranks briefly flash through my mind, but my focus remains. The music from the bars various jukebox's increases as each bar tries to outdo the other in an all out volume war. The lights in the flats opposite flash on and off unrepentantly like an 80's disco as people come and go, but the target's room is still dark, still empty.

There has been no communication with HQ for hours now and my patience is starting to wear thin. Do they know I'm still here? I'm tired, so damn tired, how long do they expect me to keep this up? I've been with the department over two years now and I'm still pulling these mindless gigs.

A fight breaks out below and the street becomes alive with violence and volume as kicks, punches, blood and bruises become the order of the day. It's only the distant sound of sirens that forces the mob to scatter. The unfortunate victim lays helpless by the kerb, blood from his shattered face flows into the street only to be washed away as the rain starts again. The mood again changes from violence to jubilation as drunken songs echo in the night as friendships are formed and relationships made.

The night's mayhem finally comes to end as the bars close in unison leaving the few remaining drunken stragglers to navigate their way home with their new found conquests. The streets can finally begin to sleep, but just as they start to doze they are roused again by the sound of the city's nocturnal cleaners removing the weekend's pavement filth. My eyelids feel heavy, my vision blurred, but there's nothing I can do. I check and recheck the equipment. The night wears on and the streets are now empty, bar one drunk sprawled over a park bench, piercing the night's glorious silence with occasional retching. I then get the call, "Price, target approaching." My pulse begins to race as I back away from the window and turn out the light. My work is about to begin.

I reach for the camera, adjust my position and wait. The target is still not in view. Waiting becomes an art: time passes; nothing changes. One eye closed, the other pressed firmly against the viewfinder as I scan the streets. The rain starts again, a light September shower helps wash away the remnants of last night's excesses. The drunk on the bench stirs, his hands rubbing his pounding head, attempting to piece together the night before. The obvious discomfort on his face shows that his surroundings are clearly a mystery to him. Not to me though, I know every inch of this place, seems like home now.

The buses have again started their endless circuit round this city, stopping only to pick up the solitary suited weekend worker. His face is the reason I stopped the nine to five rat race. "Sucker" I whisper to myself to break silence, good to hear my voice again; the one in my head sounds different. After all who's the real sucker? I'm laying on a hardwood floor, cold, tired and hungry with only a camera and a photo for company. I'm starting to wonder who smells worse the drunk or me as I catch my own stench that carries on the breeze from the open window.

The news stand on the corner opens and one by one people from the surrounding buildings scuttle over, hungry for yesterday's news. The civilian routine is now in full swing, as more people fill the street, each minding the other's business. Nobody notices the slender female shuffling nervously along the pavement. Me? I notice everything.

The photo does her no justice. She's changed since it was taken. Gone is the long auburn hair to be replaced by a savage blonde crop. Her make up is harsh and heavy, but I remember the face. She wears a long black coat wrapped tightly around her body to keep out the early morning chill. The eyes, though, they are still the same.

My camera follows her slowly across the street towards her apartment block. She appears cautious, afraid even. Something's wrong. Does she know we're onto her? How can she? Nobody on this case would have slipped. Her body language is wrong, nervous even. I'm too tired for this.

The open window frosts my breath but that morning chill keeps me alert, it's just the cold and the cramp keeping me going now. The urge to sleep is growing, no chance now, though. I reach for my cigarettes, but then think better of it; don't want to give away my position with an early morning smoke trail. My focus is drawn back to the target as I watch her approach the apartment block. She opens the entrance to the lobby and with a nervous glance left and right she glides out of sight.

The six flights of stairs she has to climb gives me the chance to stretch my limbs, need to keep the blood flowing. Need to stay alert, ready to move. Lucky for me the elevator in her block is down. I reposition and refocus on her apartment opposite. My view allows me to see two bedrooms, a small lounge and her front door.

The outside world is now blocked out and only the frame my camera gives me remains. Her door slowly opens and in she walks, softly shutting the door behind her like a teenager breaking curfew. I close in on her face, focus and start clicking.

The role of film is quick to end, never was one for digital. I reload and start snapping again, homing in on her cold loveless face. The lack of light in her flat makes me curse, wasting film with useless shots. Why keep the light off? What's she's hiding? This gloomy morning is no friend of mine.

I stare as she removes her coat and watch how it slides off her slender body onto the floor. She then kicks off her heels and heads for the sofa, collapsing onto it. Whatever she was up to last night has clearly taken its toll she's asleep within minutes.

I glance over to the kettle in the corner of this bare room, one of the only luxuries I allow myself. Experience has taught me to always be prepared; you never know how long these jobs will take. I look back at the target but she's fast asleep. So I down tools, back away from the window and flick on the kettle. Instant coffee's all I have but it will do. While the water's boiling I head to the small wash basin in the corner of this disused bed-sit and empty my bladder. Within minutes I'm back by the window hot coffee in one hand, camera in the other.

The street below is now in full swing. The shoppers scurry around darting from shop to shop in their useless futile quest for happiness. I hear the inane chatter of a hundred different conversations that are brought to my window by the strong breeze outside. The rain has subsided but the clouds outside still block the sun from making a welcome appearance. I finish the coffee, put down the cup and bring the camera back to my tired eyes. My eyes focus again on the girl asleep on the sofa. It is only then I notice the static figure hiding in the shadows in the corner of her room.

What have I missed? Panic flashes through me, damn coffee! I knew it was a bad idea. Adrenalin floods my system and sweat cascades my forehead making my eyes sting. I look again what's that flashing in their hand? A knife maybe? Now I know I'm in trouble.

Without thinking, I grab the radio and call in " Price here, target in trouble! Do you hear me? Target in danger." Nothing. "I repeat target in danger!" No response. What's going on? Where's the backup? My job is only to record, not to get involved. I look again. The figure is still there unmoving. What are they waiting for? I look back to the target. She's fast asleep on the sofa oblivious to the danger she's in. The figure then steps out of the shadow towards the sofa, knife glistening in their left hand.

The poor light in the apartment makes me squint. I can see the blade, but not the assailant's face. There's not enough light for a good shot, but it doesn't matter. A photo isn't going to help the girl. Time slows to a standstill while thoughts of my next move crackle through my tired mind like signals through faulty wiring. What to do? It's a stark choice between doing my job and heeding my conscience. Whatever I do is going to have repercussions. I look again and see in slow motion the figure getting nearer to the sofa showing no great urgency in their actions.

"Fuck this!" I curse loudly to myself breaking the claustrophobic silence that I have endured these past few days. I'm on my feet within seconds. There's a lot of ground to cover between us. It is twelve floors, six down and another six up. I drop the camera like a child's discarded toy and charge towards the door. I race down the stairs taking three at a time careful not to lose my footing. My mind is focused on speed; it's only my unwilling body that slows me down. I'm out of the building within minutes and onto the busy street.

The city fumes sear my lungs as I fight to draw breath. Too many years of bad living have caught up with me. My body is no longer willing; my burning limbs are a testament to my unwillingness to exercise.

I look across the street and focus, time is running out. The countdown ticking in my mind spurs me on.

The Saturday morning traffic is hell as I duck and weave through the oncoming cars. A chorus of car horns blare in frustration as I slow down the driver's mundane journeys. At last, I make it across the street. I feel the whole world's gaze upon me as I leave the angry drivers loudly cursing my stupidity. I continue my sprint though the throngs of shoppers, bouncing off them like a crazed pinball to reach the target's building. I get to the entrance and push the door, locked. "Shit!" I shout, causing yet more heads to turn in my direction. Panic arrives as I push and pull the door to no avail. It's only then I notice the row of buttons to my left. I blindly press them all hoping for a response. I wait a lifetime it seems for something, anything to happen. All hope leaves me as I visualise a bloody massacre upstairs.

A buzzer sounds and I push the door and to my relief it swings violently open. It closes behind me with a loud thud as I race through the lobby towards the staircase past the broken elevator. I take the stairs in no time and within minutes I'm standing outside the target's apartment, fists clenched and gasping for air.

Two

The tap, tap, tapping of rain on the corridor window unnerves me as the weather outside takes a turn for the worst. I suck in a long slow breath to calm myself I need to stay focused. I walk towards the target's door and slowly push it and watch as it slowly opens to reveal darkness. The curtains have been closed, and the lights remain off. I pause, listening for movement. Silence. I then quietly tiptoe into the room being careful not to make a sound surprise is now my only weapon. I curl up my right hand to make a fist, its only now that I realise how defenseless I truly am against a bladed assailant.

My eyes start to readjust to the darkness and the blurred shapes in front of me finally to come into focus. All is still, only the rain hammering down outside is audible.

I scan the room for signs of life, nothing. Whoever it was, they're gone now. I have a bad feeling about this. I approach the sofa, apprehensive about what I'm going to witness, I look down and my worst fears are confirmed.

Her dead eyes are open, looking to me for help, but it's too late, I wasn't quick enough. Her throat is cut, a professional single slice from ear to ear. There is blood everywhere she never had a chance, poor girl. Her mouth is slightly open as if she's trying to tell me something, like she's calling out from the dead.

The tears come unexpectedly as I collapse to the floor oblivious to the danger I could still be in. I can't bear to look at her like this with the strange smile frozen onto her lifeless face. The sobbing is uncontrollable as I'm drenched with guilt for my slow reactions, If only I had been faster, she might still be alive. How am I going to explain this to the children?

My usual senses have deserted me as I rampage through the apartment for signs of the killer. All my usual instincts gone, replaced by uncontainable grief and anger. Even as the tears continue to stream down my face, I know I got to get a hold of myself I need to think clearly. I find myself again back by the sofa looking down at the beauty that once was, and thinking about the wasted life in front of me. Her china white face is nearly unrecognisable from the one I knew.

I then notice the knife under the sofa. I reach down and pick it up. It's a slim professional blade that's sticky to touch from the blood that coats the black plastic handle. I stand there a while whilst clutching the blade white-knuckle tightly in my right hand, lost in a moment of silent frenzy.

A loud bang snaps me out of my momentary catatonia as the apartment door slams open revealing three burly uniformed police officers in full riot gear looking at me with revulsion in their eyes. They switch on the light, and there I am standing over a dead body, with a bloody knife in my right hand, and my eyes still wet from crying.

"Drop the Knife!" The smallest of the three cops shouts. The knife slips out of my hand and hits the bare floorboards. A loud metallic clang snaps me out of the daze I'm in and brings me back to the reality of my current situation. “Put your hands above your head and slowly turn around to face the wall," he continues to command, while the other two simply stare at me, waiting for their moment to get me alone, so they can dish out their own brand of justice.

I comply with his wishes whilst trying to assess the situation; there are three cops with no guns, only black handled batons. Could I overpower them? Probably, but that would really make me look guilty. I have no other option but to go with them and play the fool.

I get pushed to the wall and my legs kicked open in a blur of activity as the two silent types cuff me. “Just wait till we get you back to our house!” one of them whispers to me as he tightens the cuffs. I can faintly hear the white noise crackling of a two-way radio as the talker calls for backup.

I remain silent not wanting to goad the irate plods any further; they are already red faced and baying for blood. Inside I’m shaking, but on the surface I try to appear as cool as possible. "Any chance of a smoke?" I ask in quiet desperation.

"No chance.” They respond in unison.

I am led outside and down the six flights of stairs into the lobby of the building where two plain-clothes detectives eye me suspiciously. They look like detectives, both wearing cheap ill-fitting suits. They both scowl, as I'm lead past them onto the street. A crowd has gathered, all wanting a piece of information. Crowds always love a story, the more macabre the better. Within minutes, I'm thrown violently into a waiting police van, and the doors are locked, leaving me alone. Again.

The silence in the van is deafening as I start to comprehend the hole I'm in. I can’t seem to figure a way out. My cocky self assurance of earlier has well and truly faded now that the reality of my situation has started to sink into my sleep depraved mind. I close my eyes and try to clear my brain of the sight of her, of her bleeding corpse. I'm startled by the sound of the engine roaring to life as the van moves off. The journey doesn't take long, ten minutes at the most, and before I know it the doors are opened and I'm manhandled out of the van and into the back of the nearest precinct.

The place goes quiet when I'm brought in. 'Guilty before proven innocent' still clearly the motto in this stinking place. I get the feeling that I'm not going to get out of here in one piece. I'm pushed, pulled, punched, kicked and prodded all the way to a holding cell, where I'm thrown in, still handcuffed, battered and bruised.

I head to the corner of the cell tired and emotional and curl into a ball as the vision of her bloodied smiling face returns to haunt me. I sit there alone, with only my thoughts for company but mercifully the visions of the ghastly sights of today fade away as sleep finally overpowers me.

I wake startled from a dreamless sleep as the pain from my handcuff wrists becomes unbearable. What was going on? Why haven't I been searched yet? What's the holdup, back in my day the first twelve hours of the case was crucial, obviously these boys have got better things to do than question an ex-cop like me.

All that I could think of now was my half smoked pack of cigarettes that I left next to the camera in the tiny bed-sit, boy I sure could use both right now. The camera may be the key to my freedom and the smokes the key to my sanity.

A loud bang and the sound of a lock turning makes me spring to my feet as I suck in a deep breath ready to face whatever is coming to me. The heavy door to the cell then opens and in walks two detectives, one clearly past his sell-by date, the other barely out of nappies.

"We are ready for you now," the craggy faced detective wheezes as he leads me out of the cell and into interrogation room one. With these two on my case, I've got no hope.

I step into the room and am instantly transported back to my time with the force. Even though it's been three long years since I was last here, nothing has changed. The walls are still the nicotine stained yellow that I remember, the pot of filter coffee still bubbles away to nothing in the corner. Even the plastic seats look the same, stained with a decade's worth of scum and lies.

“Take a seat.” The kid commands and I'm quick to comply as I slump down onto the chair and rest my elbows on the table that separates me from the two detectives.

"So are you going un-cuff me?" I state casually. "You know the protocol, and I know my rights," I continue. I then nonchalantly extend my wrists in the direction of the two cops.

"All right Richard," the gray haired cop replies. He reaches for the key and pops open my cuffs instantly relieving the dull ache in my wrists. The same cop then shoots me a serious stare. "Richard, you're in real trouble," he tells me.

“Tell me something I don't know." I shoot right back.

"The media has not been alerted, and nobody knows that we have a suspect in custody; including most of the men in this building," he calmly states. "Let's call it a professional courtesy," He continues, "We had to pull a lot of strings to keep this quiet. There was quite a crowd gathered at the scene." I know what he's about to say before he does. "So just help us out on this. Tell us what you were doing there."

I take my time and study the cop's face. He's an old guy now; time has damaged him. All those years on the force have weathered the poor guy. That's what you get for spending your life on the street, nothing but an empty wallet, wrinkles, and a bottle for company.

"Come on, Richard! It doesn't look good for you, does it? You need to help us help you. Make it easy on yourself," he tells me. It's the standard cop patter. I've heard it a hundred times. I know these guys want a collar, and they want it all for themselves. That's why they snuck me in here, and why the act. Who do they take me for? The chance to bang up an ex-cop like me, it's like a dream come true for these guys, especially with our past history.

I contemplate telling them about the camera, but I know that would be a bad idea. I don't trust the cops in this city to do the right thing; it's all too easy for evidence to go missing. I take a long slow breath and think, I've got to contact the department; they'll get me out of this.

"Come on Rich, times running out before we have to charge you," the old cop reminds me. "We might be able to get you out of this mess if you tell us what happened," he continues to lie.

"I'll tell you everything you want to know," I reply. I then pause for a moment, and look towards the door, "You know me, anything to help. However before I start; I could kill for a cup of coffee and a cigarette."

The younger of the two cops stands. "Sure thing Rich," he mutters and leaves the room with the door left open behind him.

I sit in silence, trying not to meet the older cop's gaze as we wait for my coffee. The silence is broken when a young fresh faced beat cop pokes his head in. "Adams, there's someone at the front desk asking for you. They say it's urgent," he announces.

"Shit," comes the reply. "Sorry, Rich, I'll be as quick as possible. I want this over as quickly as you," he tells me before he follows the younger man out of the door.

The door closes behind them, and in an instant, I'm on my feet. I head straight to the door and try it. It opens - the fool forgot to lock it. "I'm not going to wait around to get screwed," I tell myself as I slip out of the interview room and head along the corridor. No one pays me any attention as I calmly walk through the freshly bleached corridor, down the stairs, and out through the back door. I tense up as I pass a small group of cops who are indulging in a cigarette break like naughty schoolboys. I get the impression that they are more worried that I'm going to make a comment about them smoking on duty than about me. I walk on out through the yard and out onto the street. It's only then that I start running.

I make straight for the river that cuts this city open like a knife. It's a good place to disappear. I can't go home, that’s for sure. I still live in the same apartment that I had when I was on the force, so they are bound to have the address. I need a place to lay low and think. I also need to go and retrieve the camera, but that'll have to wait. The area will be swarming with cops, and by now they are all going to be pissed off and looking for me.

I think back to my time on the force, trying to rack my brains for a name; someone I could trust, but no ordinary police ever trusted internal affairs. The Rat-Squad was always treated with more contempt than most felons. There was no hope to be found going down that avenue, the chances of finding good police, someone willing to believe me, were slim to none. I was on my own

At last, I reach the river and finally start to relax, as the familiar tidal smells filled my nostrils. It's good to be back on familiar ground. It's beginning to get dark. I needed somewhere to hole up for the night, somewhere out of sight. I rummage through my pockets, but all I can find is a well-used credit card. I head to the nearest ATM, and withdraw as much as I can. I need to get out of the area, so I cross the river, and head towards the safety of the East End.

I walk along the river's embankment, so I can get lost in the evening's crowd. I need to stay on foot I don't want to get caught on camera somewhere. If they are going to find me, it won't be due to my stupidity.

The sun finally disappears over the horizon, and the city lights come alive. I watch the light's reflection bounce around on the surface of the river's slow moving current. I keep walking, using the river to guide me to the East End. The temperature drops as I walk and before I realise it I'm shaking. I need to get out of this cold and wind. "It's not far to go, now," I tell my poor aching body.

I take a left turn, leaving the river and the breeze from the sea behind me. I head to the old part of town; somewhere I can vanish. At last, the old tenement buildings of the East End come into view, and I finally start to feel safer. I keep my eyes open, looking for a place to crash; somewhere that no questions will be asked.

I see the perfect place in front of me; a run down terrace hotel squeezed between and liquor store and a do it yourself launderette. The glowing purple neon lit sign swings slowly in the breeze and to my relief it's advertising vacancies.

Outside the building, a couple stand arguing at first I take it for a lovers tiff, but as I got closer it's clearly a pimp at work. "Perfect," I mutter to myself, nobody will look for me here. I climb the three steps that lead into the building, and head straight for the desk. An old, white haired man, with near yellow skin and matching teeth suspiciously glares at me as he removes the cigarette that has been dangling out of the corner of his mouth.

"Hour, or the night?" He calmly asks.

"Night," I reply as I hand him a bundle of cash. He doesn't ask for a name, and I don't give one. He unhooks a key from the rack behind him and slides it across the mock wooden desk.

“Number 14 up the stairs, second left, enjoy your stay,” he tells me in a craggy half mocking tone.

"Cheers," is my sullen reply.

The room itself is everything I expected; damp, dank, and untidy. The sheets look soiled, the carpet filthy, but it will do for now. I leave the light off and head straight to the unmade double bed and remove the damp and soiled sheets, leaving them in a pile by the door. Once all traces of the previous guests have been removed, I collapse onto the bare mattress. It's too late to do anything now, I'm too damn tired. My brain aches and pulses with a mixture of nerves and exhaustion. The street outside is quiet, except for the buzzing of the faulty, neon sign outside my window that continually buzzes on and off. The events of the last few days run through my mind as I drift off into welcome oblivion.

I awake confused, not knowing when or where I am. The sun streams through the giant holes in the curtains burning my tired eyes. The acrid smell then hits me as my senses go into overload. Half blind and with a nose full of stink, I take a look at my surroundings in the cold light of day. The wallpaper is peeling off the walls, and there are damp patches where pictures should be.

I glance at the cheap watch on my wrist. It reads 3:48pm. "Shit!" I curse, ruing that I had already wasted half of the day. I head to what can loosely be called a bathroom, and take a welcome shower. I feel the hot water cascading over my stale body, but I don't feel any cleaner. It will take more than hot water to wash away the things I've seen.

Once I'm done, I slowly change back into my well-worn clothes. I sit back on the bed, and try to think. I need a plan of action, as I try to snap myself out of the inescapable depression that's lurking in my subconscious; I need to be pro-active. First things first, I need to contact the firm, and let them know what happened. That should give me a break from the law. Then, hopefully, I can retrieve the camera; it's all the evidence I need. Then I'm going to find the bastard who killed her.

I'm now ready to face the day, my plan is set. I get to my feet and head out of the room. "Hope you enjoyed your stay," the old man calls out as I walk through the door onto the street.

“Delightful,” I call back sarcastically.

I notice the news stand on the corner of the street, and head towards it, while fumbling in my pocket for change. I approach the vender, and ask for the morning tabloid and then realise that my life as I know it is now over. The blood red headline sends a wave of nausea through my tight knotted gut and it takes every ounce of strength for me to suck it back and appear calm and as I casually walk away from the kiosk. "Ex-cop rapes and kills wife," The headline goes round and round my fragile eggshell brain. I suck in a sharp intake of breath, and look again at the front page and stare in disbelief at the picture of me in full police uniform staring back at me.

I close the paper rapidly, and start to walk. The sound of a humming exhaust in the distance doesn't sound right and causes me to quicken my pace. I look behind and see two squad cars silently moving towards the hotel. It looks like the receptionist also read the papers this morning. I continue to walk quickly, not wanting to draw attention to myself. I try to remain calm, though I'm screaming inside.

I have to get off the streets, and wait for the night to disguise me. The whole of this damned stinking city is going to be looking for me now. I have got to hide, to disappear, and right now only one place comes to mind. Skid Row, even the cops don't go there. I have no option but to walk it. Luckily, I know this city better than I know myself.

I head back to the river still clutching the morning's tabloid in my hand and walk along its murky banks. Time feels irrelevant as I walk by the river into the city's once great industrial area. The only noise I hear is the humming from the factories to my left. The various workers, on their smoke breaks, pay no attention to me as I scuttle past. To my right is the canal. It's an offshoot from the river, which once was the main transport from the factories to the docks. It's now used more as a dumping ground for household waste. The more I walk, the further into Skid Row I get. There are disused buildings all over the area, the last remnants of this city's great industrial heritage.

This is where the dregs of society come, the unwell, the junkies, the lushes the homeless. They all gather together where nobody else can see them, out of society's gaze. If they can't be seen; they don't exist. Nobody will come looking for me here. It's the perfect place to lay low.

I spy a small outhouse by the canal, by the looks of it it was once a coal shed, that fuelled the barges that once used this canal like cars on a motorway. It had now fallen into ruin. The windows are boarded and the old oak door is so rotten it is a miracle that it's still upright. The door creaks open with just a slight tug. Inside the smell hits me square on the nose like an unexpected blow from a prize fighter. In the corner of the dank room sits a mouldy mattress covered with old newspapers. The floor is littered with old food cartons and beer cans. It is obviously a home for somebody, but it'll suit my needs perfectly. The various holes in the roof allow me enough light to be able to shut the door behind me. I clear a corner of the room and take a seat on the cold concrete floor. I open the newspaper and begin to read the full story.

The reporting in the paper bares no relation to the actual events. Jessica left me seven years ago, but the story makes out that we were in the process of a separation, claiming that was the motivation for my attack. I start to wonder where this reporter got his facts. He describes the murder scene to a tee; perhaps he was fed this information. It claims they have only one suspect, and pretty much declares me guilty. The more I read, the angrier I get. I look to the bottom of the story and spot the reporter's name, "J. Fitzgerald." It was a name I recognised. Mr Fitzgerald was in the pay of the Police and always printed what he was told.

I put down the paper, and wait for darkness. The wind outside begins to pick up, and makes the old roof groan. The rain begins, and I watch the leaky roof deliver water in drips towards the floor. All I can do now is wait, rest, and plan my next move.

Three

The light outside finally fades and night makes a welcome return. I stand up and brush myself down. Outside I hear the shuffling of feet. The front door opens with a slight pull and I walk out into the cold bitter night. I feel refreshed and renewed, one thing’s for sure, I’m done hiding, done running.

The slum is starting to fill with the city's down and outs, making their way here to escape the night. I watch as they shuffle towards shelter like zombies, oblivious to my presence. One tramp hobbles past me clutching a bottle of spirits, lost in booze. The stench and degradation of this place makes my eyes sting. I don't want to end up here. I don’t want this life, this lonely existence, away from the world, away from humanity.

I need to head south, across the river to the department, its time I started fighting back. I head back towards the river, through the East End, and into Soho. The beard growing on my face makes me itch but also helps to disguise me. Nobody pays me any attention as I walk through the neon seediness of Soho. The city’s thrill seekers flock here night after night in search of drugs, girls and good times. They tend to leave with an empty wallet and a head full of shame. Me? Tonight I just look like another down and out. It’s funny how the homeless have a way of simply disappearing.

The buildings round here are all clip joints, bars and fast food restaurants. Well, that's what they claim to be, but I'm not so sure. I keep my eyes down as I walk, trying not to arouse any suspicions. The Soho cut through brings me back towards the embankment and the river.

The old steel suspension bridge that crosses the river comes into view and I head towards it. My feet start to ache as I pound the asphalt. The bridge is busy tonight, full of traffic heading south and out of this god-forsaken town.

I see the building I'm looking for - a small modern block, full of blacked out windows facing out towards the river. It sits a little back from the river. It is one of those buildings that's easy to miss if you're not looking for it, as it sits nestled in between a large banking corporation and medieval stone church. The entrance is located on the south side, away from the water and the bright lights.

I approach and casually open the door that leads me into the building's reception area. I walk through the red-carpeted lobby, passing the unmanned front desk, and head towards the elevators. All is unusually quiet as I step into the lift and press the button for the third floor. I feel nervous, it's too quiet, where is everybody? I reach my floor and march towards my tiny office. The door has an electronic lock with a four-digit key pass. I enter the code and the lock buzzes as I push it open.

The place is bare. The battered computer that once sat atop of the metal desk has gone, along with the filing cabinet that contained all my past cases. All that remains of my time here is the desk and leather swivel chair, it was like I was never here.

The mechanical whirring of the lift outside breaks my concentration and I poke my head into the corridor, watching the light above the lift come to a stop on the three. Someone's coming. I step back into the office, and close the door softly behind me. Careful not to make any noise, I press my right ear up to the cold, pine door and listen to the soft footsteps exiting the lift. I hold my breath as the footsteps pass me and carry on down the hallway towards the records room.

There's no time to think. I need answers; it is now or never. I open the door, and follow the source of the footsteps, careful not to alert anyone to my presence. The opening and closing of a filing cabinet breaks the sweaty silence as I continue to creep towards the source of the noise.

The records room is located in the last room at the far end of the corridor. The door is ajar and I see the shape of a young woman, her back turned as she's hunched over a filing cabinet. She has long, natural blonde hair that is tied back. Her attire is that of a professional, a secretary perhaps. She must be new, because I don't recognise her, but then, I never was in the office that much. At any rate, this is one broad that I would have definitely remembered.

A single bulb on a bare wire hangs from the aertex ceiling, illuminating this dingy space. The woman is too engrossed in her work to notice me creep towards the light switch and flick it off. The light cuts out and the room is bathed in darkness. "Who's there?" The woman's shrill small voice calls out. She nervously fumbles her way towards the switch with one hand outstretched, the other clutching the file that she was in the middle of reading.

I take a deep breath; like lightning I make my move. I step forward through the darkness and grab the dame tightly. One hand reaches across her mouth, the other around her slim body. I pull her away from the switch and the door. She tries to scream but my hand tightens over her mouth, muffling her shrill little voice. The last thing I need now is to alert the building's security. I'm too strong for her as she thrashes her body against mine in a desperate attempt to escape. Dropping her paperwork all over the floor, she struggles to break free from my vice like grip. "I'm not going to hurt you," I whisper softly in her ear. She winces as my stubble burns her face in the ongoing struggle.

"I just want answers," I reassure her. "I'm going to move my hand, so don't scream. Do you understand?" She nods her head in acknowledgement. I release my grip over her mouth, but continue to hold her body close. I don't want to chase this dame. "What do you want?" her shrill, little voice nervously asks.

"Answers, just answers," my dry croaky voice replies.

The woman in my grip shudders from nerves as I hold her firmly against my body. "I'm going to let go now, don't try to run," I warn her, using the sternest voice I can muster. "Do you understand?" She nods her sweaty head in agreement. I look towards the closed door and I calculate the possibility of the woman making a run for it. There's no chance she would make it past me, so I relax my grip on her.

Once she feels the pressure loosening she squirms out of my arms and stumbles a few feet towards the window. Her breathing is fast and shallow; she's clearly in shock. I watch as she attempts to compose herself. She uses the tinted window as a mirror to adjust her ponytail, which, in the struggle, has slipped to the left. Once she has calmed down and is satisfied that her appearance is of its usual high standard, she turns round to face me.

"So what do you want?" She calmly asks trying to impose a sense of authority. "My office, down the hall, it's empty, all my stuff's gone, files, personal items the works, and I want to know why?" She looks confused and dazed by the question, obviously not what she was expecting. She must have taken me for a robber or a rapist.

"Mr, you've got the wrong girl, I'm just a file clerk. I can't help you, besides I've only been here two weeks," her shrill little voice replies. Trust me to kidnap the only person in the whole building who knows less than me, a bloody office junior.

"If you are a clerk, please can you show me where all the personnel files are kept?" I politely ask trying to put the poor girl at ease.

"Okay," she stutters nervously. She then walks over to a beat up filing cabinet in the corner of the room and slides open a drawer. "What name should I be looking for?" she asks.

"Price. Richard Price."

The girl starts ploughing her way through a mass of files while quietly cursing under her breath. It feels like an age as she checks then re-checks. I watch, slightly amused, as she appears to get more and more flustered. She obviously does not want to give me bad news. "Sorry mister, there's nothing under that name here," she stutters. The Bambi-eyed look she throws me puts me at ease, and I walk towards the cabinet in an attempt to look myself.

I brush her aside, looking down at the open cabinet and start searching. Nothing. "They must have moved my file."

"Look mister I don't know who you are or what you want, but I can't help you," she tells me.

"Where else would the files be?" I question.

"They should all be here" she replies.

The girl looks at me, waiting for me to say or do something. I pause for a moment lost in thought; I need to work out my next move. It's clear to me that my personnel files have been removed - they have clearly removed all traces of me ever working here. Why though? What are they hiding?

I'm so lost in thought that I don't notice her move. The knee she uses to crush my groin comes from nowhere. All the wind rushes out of my lungs as I crumple to the ground. The unexpected hammer blow brings tears to my eyes as I try to focus on what just happened.

The lady then attacks again expertly kicking me again in the baby maker. I double up on the floor trying to protect the area from her powerful well-heeled blow. She's no clerk, the only thought coursing through my mind as I unsuccessfully try to dodge the third blow. I'm unable to move through shear pain, and I have no choice but to watch as she runs to retrieve a file from one of the cabinets. She then opens the door and silently makes her way out of the room. Just before she disappears, she turns to face me and blows me a kiss.

The searing pain in my loins will act as a good reminder never to let my guard down again. Whoever she was, she was good, had me fooled. No doubt she's contacted the building's security or even the Police. Despite the pain I have to move, I have to get out of this damn building.

I haul myself to my feet, turn towards the window and look out towards the street for any sign of the police. I'm in luck its deathly quiet outside. I try to stand but my legs are in agony, as a shooting pain from my nervous system transports bolts of agony all throughout my lower body. I try to focus on what just happened but the events are a blur in my mind. What was she doing here? Was it connected to me? What was it she was after?

The pain in my groin finally subsides, and I rush over to the cabinet she was at and slide it towards me and peer down at the files. "Sneaky bitch," I mutter to myself as I come across the personnel files I was looking for earlier, my file. I pull out the A4 brown envelope and open it but to my horror, it's empty. I open the cabinet again and replace the empty file and a familiar name catches my eye. I look down again and notice a file with her name on it "Mrs J Price." A little out of date, I think to myself. To my frustration those contents have also been removed. What the hell is going on?

I have been here too long; I need to get out of the building. It's only a matter of time before that honey reports the incident and then I'm in real trouble. I take one last look at the room and to my surprise, I spot a small black leather handbag lying forgotten below the light switch. I bend down and grab the bag before turning off the light and leaving the room for the last time.

All is quiet as I retrace my steps along the garishly carpeted corridor towards the stairs. I'm nearly to the bottom when I hear voices in the lobby. Reaching the door that separates the stairs from the lobby, I press my ear against the cold steel door. It's difficult to make out what's being said, thanks to the thickness of the fire door and the whispered conversation.

"He never struck me as the type," I hear a nasal voice state.

“Luke, you watch far too much TV, I’m telling you it can’t be healthy, you’re starting to sound like you actually know these people. You do realise it’s just a show?” A second voice replies as I listen to their inane late night conversation.

The voices then become too muffled to understand. I then hear the sound of footsteps leaving the lobby. At least I know whose on the other side of the door I think to myself. The burly bald headed night security officer always was one for TV gossip. I had always put it down to loneliness. This building has always been pretty quiet at night, so he always did welcome any conversation be it gossip or otherwise. The other voice though I cannot place, although I guess it to be the mawkish pencil thin cleaner that I occasionally saw loitering in the building. I keep my ear pressed to the door but there's nothing more to be heard. I suspect the cleaner has continued on his rounds while the guard is probably sitting back in his chair by the entrance to the building.

It's been a hell of a day I consider as I look back on the past twenty-four hours, why me? I swing open the door and march purposefully across the lobby. The guard nearly falls off his chair in disbelief, my face clearly familiar to him. He can’t quite believe what he's seeing as I head straight to the door. He then leaps up and heads my way. "You better stop there," he shouts at me. I keep walking. I watch as his hand reaches towards his baton by his side and he runs towards me. Who’s he fooling? I'm twenty younger and a good thirty pounds lighter than him.

He lunges towards me, baton in hand. I expertly sidestep his attack and watch how he clumsily topples over my outstretched leg and lands with a heavy thud on the carpet. Within a flash I'm outside the building and heading off into the night, even before the security guard has worked out what hit him. It's now time to get the camera, the Bambi-eyed girl and some answers.

Four

My eyes sting as a strong crisp breeze blows right at me from across the river. I reach out and grab the rail of the bridge as I slowly make my way across it. I clutch the black leather handbag tightly into my chest as I fight my way through the wind and over the grey river. I look to the sky and see the stars through the city's murky haze and watch as the evening blooms. I have no doubt as to my next move. I try to look menacing as a few cars slow down to stare at the sight of a man with a handbag being beaten up by the breeze, but lucky for me none recognise my felonious face.

It doesn't take long for me to navigate my way through the back streets of this smoky neon lit city to the West End. The streets are near empty now as the moon signals an end to the city's trading hours. Only the town's underclass's can be seen loitering, some asleep in shop doorways, others hunting like wolves for leftovers in the bins that line the streets. The pavements are awash with piss and booze, which I sidestep as I make my way back towards the bed-sit, back to the camera.

I criss-cross the streets heading back towards the stakeout location where all this trouble started. The back of my legs ache as the West End's shopping district comes into view. It's deserted now; only the cleaners remain, working hard at preparing the shops for the following day's trade. I then see the familiar bus shelter come into view as I approach the building where I spent those three long days.

I look towards the building where she died, and for a moment I'm lost in grief and guilt. My eyes flick back towards the building on my right, while I try to suppress the rage that I feel. Revenge has now become my friend and my motivation.

I reach the old oak door and push it open revealing cold stone stairs that lead up to the empty apartment. It takes a matter of minutes to climb the six flights and before long I'm back at the apartment door. I stand outside, take a deep breath and slowly push it open. The door makes a loud squeak, as its rusty hinges swing into action.

A wave of relief hits me as I spot the camera laying abandoned on the floor with only an empty coffee cup next to it for company. It's clear that no one has been here since I left. I head over towards my trusted friend and scoop him up, then flip him over and see that the roll of film is still snugly in place. Mission accomplished.

The ache in my legs and groin reminds me that it's time to rest. I grab the empty cup, head over to the corner of this barren apartment and make myself some rancid coffee. Once the drink is made, I collapse onto the floor and slowly sip the foul smelling liquid masquerading as coffee.

I finally open the bag that I've carried all this way and rummage. A purse, lip-gloss, make up - all the usual accruements of a lady's handbag. As I open the purse to empty it of cash, I see what I'm looking for her driver's license. Bingo! I now have a name and address for that sweet Bambi-eyed girl.

The moon is gloating at the earth as it sits high above the storm clouds that gather menacingly above the city. I'm tired. I need to get my head down and recharge, it's going to be a busy night. I rest my head on the bare floorboards and slowly drift off to sleep watching the grey clouds being blown violently across the sky.

The sound of thunder startles me from my slumber. The weather outside is blowing hard, I watch as the street litter is picked up and carried away by the strong breeze. The black clouds that are dropping their wet load indiscriminately across this dirty old town obscure the sinking moon.

My watch tells me dawn is approaching, although it's hard to tell by looking out of the window. I'm going to wait until the storm clears before I make my move. I look again at the address 182 Weak Street; it's not far from here. It'll take me no more than an hour to walk it if I cut through the financial district. The rumble in my stomach reminds me that I have not eaten for days; it can even be heard over the sounds of the storm outside. I'll grab something on the way, I tell myself hoping that the lie will stop my guts from aching.

I refill my cup with coffee and wait. It doesn’t take long for the storm to blow out of town and into the countryside; it's time for me to leave. I pick myself up off the floor, grab the camera and expertly remove the precious roll of film inside, slipping it securely into my pocket. I won't need the camera tonight so I carefully put it back on the floor and prepare to leave.

There are few early morning shoppers on the street; lucky for me they're too caught up in the hunt for next season’s fashion to notice me. I catch my reflection in a shop window and barely recognise myself, my gaunt face is hidden by a weeks worth of dark stubble. My clothes creased and dirty, I'm starting to disappear. I spot flashing blue lights up ahead and calmly cross the street and walk past the police as they struggle with a would-be bag thief.

The journey through the city is over in a flash; my mind is filled with thoughts of my next move. I need to get information from her, but I've got to be careful, I won't make the same mistake twice. I look up at the rusty bent street sign. "Weak Street." I'm here at last.

The street is full of modern houses and new luxury apartments, a soulless place, the kind of place where loud brash city boys with their blue shirts and power suits live. This area is part of this great city's expansion plans as it slowly eats its way into the ever-decreasing countryside. Like all else in this world, they only cater to the rich, and the homeless are left with only doorways for shelter.

I cross the street and follow the house numbers until I reach my destination - 182. It's a smallish house that's squeezed between two apartment blocks. It's a two up, two down affair with a small wall that separates it from the street. I also notice a gate to the side of the house, my entrance.

The place is dark save for a soft light coming from an upstairs window. I quietly clamber over the wall and make my way towards the gate. It opens with a single push and I check the street before I head through, softly closing it behind me.

The narrow alley that separates the two buildings is only illuminated by the orange glow of the streetlight. I follow it as it leads into a tiny paved garden at the back of the house. I then spot the back door that leads into the kitchen. The door itself is weather beaten with old red paint peeling off in places. I give it a gentle push, locked. However, I know that a good strong kick would gain me access in a matter of seconds. The kitchen window's no help, it's too dark to see anything clearly. If she is in, then it's my guess that she's asleep.

I retrace my steps and back towards the front of the house, time for play is over. This time I mean business.

. There's no peephole, even better. I bang loudly on the door and wait. Nothing. I bang again. A light comes on from the upstairs window. I bang a third time. I hear the sound of gentle footsteps coming down the stairs, "Hold on! I'm coming," a sleepy voice calls out. I recognise the voice. Perfect.

I take a step back ready to make my move. I hear the sounds of bolts being moved and keys turning. The door then slowly opens inwards. I kick it violently and let the force do the work. The door slams against the girl behind it sending her flying across the hallway. I then enter the house and quickly close the door behind me.

The girl is sprawled out on the hallway, dazed and confused. A red mark is visible on her pale forehead where the door floored her. I walk over and crouch down beside her. "Remember me?" I casually ask as she loses consciousness.

The Bambi-eyed girl's slender body is easy to move as I scoop her up and climb the stairs. I find the bedroom and fling her body onto the double bed, where a few moments ago she was resting peacefully. The room itself is a garish affair, all pink and white, more a girl's room than a woman's.

In the corner of the room sits a small portable television, it's on, but the volume is turned off. I get the feeling that this broad is tough on the outside, but weak in the middle. It looks like she's scared of the dark.

On the other side of the room sits what looks like a month's worth of dirty laundry, obviously not a top priority to this girl. I notice a heap of bras lying abandoned on the floor. "Perfect," I mutter to myself as I bend down to pick two of them up. Bras in hand, I walk over to the bed and use them to tie the girl's hands and legs tightly to the bedposts. She's not getting away this time.

The girl is breathing softly, there's no danger that she's going to be waking any time soon. A brief pang of guilt shoots through me as I look at the lump on her pretty little head; it soon vanishes as I remember the swift nut-cruncher she bestowed upon me. Now we're even.

It's now time to look around. I leave the pink bedroom and head back to the landing. The next room is tiny, more of a cupboard that a bedroom. It's full of clothes scattered indiscriminately and not much else. Jeez this girl's messy. The last room upstairs is a poorly decorated bathroom, white tiles and a maroon suite. The sink is surrounded by all manner of creams, gels and sprays, looks like a witches den to me. The downstairs is much the same, awful decor strewn with unwashed clothes. I find the kitchen and instinctively open the fridge. To my delight I find the remnants of yesterdays take-away pizza, well I hope it was yesterdays. It's gone in seconds.

The banging upstairs refocuses my attention and I make my way back to the girl and away from the fridge. The girl is now waking slowly, the look in her eye shows she's clearly not pleased to see me. I sit on the corner of the room and watch as she slowly regains consciousness. "Good evening" I tell her.

"What's so good about it?" she sarcastically replies.

"This time sweetheart I want answers, real answers."

“I don't know anything."

"You said that last time, this time it's not going to wash," I retort.

I watch as she thrashes around on the bed trying to untie herself from her bonds. "You're not going anywhere until I get what I want" I tell her menacingly. I look over to her white flat pack bedside cabinet and notice the red pack of cigarettes. "Do you mind?" I ask nodding towards the pack.

"Be my guest."

I spark up the cigarette and take a deep lungful and hold it enjoying the burning in my lungs. I then slowly exhale and savour the taste. It's been too long.

“Hey Mister, I'm still here," the girls whiney voice snaps me out of my moment.

"Are you ready to tell me what I want?" I ask.

"You're not getting it are you? I don't know who you are or what you're on about. I'm getting the feeling that you’re some kind of pervert, bursting into girls houses and tying them up," she tells me in her most innocent voice she can muster.

"Oh you know all about me alright, after all you were looking through my files," I tell her.

"I don't know what you're on about Mister," she claims, throwing me dumb look.

"Well its about time you start talking." I watch as she clams up. It’s clear that she does not intend to say a thing.

I raise the cigarette to my mouth and gently blow on it to reveal the burning orange glow of the tip. "You better start yakking," I warn as I slowly lower the burning cigarette towards her exposed stomach.

The scared look in her eyes shows me that my bluff is working. There’s no way I could really hurt this dame. I just don't have it in me, although it's clear by her expression that she doesn't know that. "Are you ready to talk yet?" I ask as I bring the cigarette closer.

"Wh-what do you want to know?" She stutters.

"First off what did you want with my file?" I ask. I watch as a small piece of ash falls from my cigarette and lands on her exposed marble belly.

"I was just doing my job. I was told to destroy all records of your time with the department," she replies with a look of fear in her eyes.

"Why?"

"I don't think the department really wanted to be seen to be employing a murderer and rapist. The last thing we need is the press snooping around it puts all our jobs at risk."

I take a long drag on the cigarette and look right in her eyes. "So they tossed me aside, to save being exposed?" I question.

“You got it,” she tells me.

Something is not right, the department has always looked after its own, no matter what. I don't buy this explanation. There has got to be more to it. It's a government run and funded department; they could hide anything if they wanted. What were they so worried about? I get the feeling that this girl knows more than what she's letting on. They don't employ street fighters like her to destroy files, although I'll play along with her see where it leads me.

"Why was I sent on the stakeout? What did the department want with Jess?" I enquire.

"I don't know, I was just instructed to destroy both your files," she explains.

"Both?" I query.

"Yes, you and Jess" she confirms.

"Where was Jess's file?"

"Same as yours, personnel."

"Jess didn't work for the department, did she?"

"Well that's were I found it." She replies. She clearly didn't mean to tell me that. I wonder what else she really knows?

"Who gave you your orders, who's your boss?"

"Paul, Paul Stewart" she mumbles.

"Interesting. It turns out we both have or should I say had the same boss" I tell her. This girl's real good, a body to die for, quick-witted and a lethal kick to boot. It's just such a shame that I don't trust her.

"Are you going to release me?" She asks throwing me the lost little girl look.

"All in good time Victoria."

Its Vicky" she corrects.

"All in good time. Vicky."

I leave her tied to the bed as I make my way across the hall towards the bathroom. It's been an age since I washed. I just need to feel human again. I strip to the waist and use the razor left lying by the side of the bath to hack the beard off my face, all the while thinking about the beautiful girl tied up in the next room. I know she's not telling me everything, but she thinks she's doing the right thing. All credit to her I suppose, after all I'm meant to be the bad guy.

There’s still one thing that bothers me. Why remove my files in the dead of night? I'm starting to wonder what Mr. Stewart is up to. One thing’s for sure; I know that Vicky will lead me straight to him.

Five

It feels great to be clean as I wash away the last few days' filth, I'm starting to feel human again; all I need now are some clean clothes. I head back to the spare room and rummage through the pile of discarded clothes looking for something to wear. Fashion is the least of my worries as I pick out a black tee shirt and an oversize pair of combat trousers. The clothes feel great against my weary skin as I head back to Vicky. I can't help but admire my skinny body as I pass by the large mirror on the landing.

I head back towards the bedroom. "Sorry about that leaving you alone Vicky, I was in real need of a wash and some fresh clothes."

"You're telling me," she jokes.

I reach for the pack of cigarettes and casually slip them into my pocket. "You don't mind, I hope. I think I need them more than you," I tell her.

"So are you going to release me? This is becoming real uncomfortable," she tells me.

"Sure" I reply.

I walk over to the bed and sit down beside her. "Roll over for me honey," I ask. Without speaking she slowly rolls over and I untie the bra releasing her hands. "I'll leave you to untie the rest," I tell her as I quickly stand up and head towards the bedroom door. "See you later," I say as I walk out of the room and head downstairs.

The front door squeaks as I close it behind me. It's still dark outside and there's a wicked chill in the air as I jog across the road and make my way towards the parked cars that line the street. The first two cars are no good but the third holds promise, it's an old Ford Escort, at least ten years old and electric blue in colour. The owner is clearly careless, as the passenger side window is not fully shut. The gap is just big enough to accommodate my arm as I reach through and quickly open the door. I get into the car and shimmy over to the driver's seat; my time on the streets serves me well as I prepare the car for ignition.

The view across the street is perfect as I get comfortable and wait for Vicky to make her move. It's just a matter of time before she runs to her boss, and I'll be right behind her.

The minutes feel like hours as I wait and watch, just like old times. There's no movement; all the lights in the house are just like I left them. She must have gone back to bed, either that or it takes her an age to get ready. I look to the sky and see that morning is soon to make a welcome appearance. There is also a slow trickle of commuters who are leaving their houses suited and ready for the office rat race. The more I see the nine to five junkies the more I start to yearn for their simple life.

I'm roused from my daydream when a light flickers off in her bedroom. I slide further down the seat so as not to be seen and keep my eyes focused on the wing mirror's reflection. The front door of her house finally opens and out she steps, dressed to kill. Her blonde hair is slightly curled and bounces seductively around her exposed shoulders. The tiny black cocktail dress and matching shoes she's wearing are no defence against the morning chill, although the sight of her all dressed up makes me forget about the cold.

I watch as she crosses the road whilst trying to apply the last of her make up. She approaches a silver two-seater Mazda 30 yards in front of me and slides into it, slamming the door behind her. I expertly hotwire the Ford car and bring it roaring into life as the Mazda pulls out into the road with me following discreetly behind it.

The morning rush hour is in full swing as more and more cars enter the fray. It's perfect for me as my car gets lost in the cascade of motor vehicles all heading into the heart of the city. I taste the fumes from the slow moving cars as I sit in traffic, my eyes firmly fixed on the Mazda in front of me. The constant stop, start, stop, start gives me a headache. It's a real shame what the traffic has done to this city. I stare out of the window and look at all the black petrol stained buildings - our heritage going up in smoke, all for convenience.

I breathe a sigh of relief when we finally pass the financial district and the traffic starts to thin out, making this tail job a little easier. Vicky is still a good three cars in front completely oblivious to my presence. Up ahead by the old Cinema I see the traffic lights changing. It's no good I'm not going to make it through without causing attention.

"Shit!" I curse loudly to myself as I watch the Mazda glide across the busy intersection while I grind to a halt waiting for the damn lights to give me green. I tap the steering wheel loudly in frustration as I watch a greasy grey bearded guy with a yellow bucket approach my car and attempt to clean the windshield. The brown water he uses only makes my visibility worse but I just ignore him and keep the window closed. He soon gets the message and runs over to another car behind mine and tries his luck again.

The lights finally change and I speed across the road and follow the direction of the Mazda. I calmly scan the street for any sign of her; she could not have gone far. Then to my relief I spot her car parked awkwardly on the pavement right outside a small coffee house. I continue driving and park fifty yards up the road, keeping my eyes firmly on the wing mirror as I wait and watch.

The weather’s warming up, looks like its going to be a sunny day, a good day for a drive. It's been a while since I've seen the sun and I momentarily forget my troubles as I wind down the window of my car and breathe in the heat of this glorious city. The loud roar of a police siren in the distance reminds me of my current predicament. I briefly consider just driving away somewhere out of this city to begin a new life; it would be easy to slip away somewhere and start again. The thought of Jess with her throat slit stops me. I will find her killer and the truth.

The sight of Vicky heading back to her car coffee cup in hand spurs me back into action as I reach for the loose wires under the steering wheel and fire the engine back into life. She slips seductively back into the car and readjusts the mirrors. I watch as she touches up her make up and finishes her drink. Finally she starts up the engine and pulls out into the street.

Her Mazda finally passes me but I wait briefly before pulling out so there are a couple of cars between us. I follow her towards the river where we cross the bridge and head south to the outskirts of the city, towards the affluent suburbs.

We drive for a good forty minutes criss-crossing the residential streets before she pulls onto a picturesque street, which the street sign tells me is called Cherry Tree Rise. The road is lined on both sides by small trees still bearing there pinkish flowing blossoms while the houses are all large and detached. It's clearly a place of some wealth; a multitude of high performance cars littering the drives and pavements confirms my suspicions that this is a place of real money.

I slow the car to a near standstill and watch as Vicky indicates before she pulls into a large sweeping drive fifty yards in front of me. I pull the Ford towards the curb and kill the engine. I wait a few minutes for Vicky to disappear out of sight before I slowly get out the car and make my way towards her parked car.

Six

The car is parked in the drive of a large detached red brick house with clearly too many rooms to count. The ivy that creeps up one side of the house gives it a mock rustic look. On the fancy paved drive I notice four cars, including Vicky's, parked haphazardly. The large oak front door is adorned with an oversized brass knocker and also a button, which I assume is an electric bell. There's no way I'm going to be able to sneak in via the front so I slowly make my way round the side of this imposing building.

Access to the side of the house is blocked by a large iron gate, I try to push it open but it's firmly locked in place. It's clear that whoever lives here is really into home security. This is going to be harder than I expected.

There's no way that I'm going to be able to scale the gate without being seen or damaging myself; I've got to find another way in. I silently jog back to the street and head quickly towards the neighbour's house, walking through their immaculately landscaped gardens. I spot a wooden gate on the left of the house and walk towards it. To my relief, it opens with a simple push. I close the gate behind me and tiptoe towards the garden. It's lucky for me its still only 9:30AM; most of the street's residents should be at work by now.

The garden has a huge green lawn that stretches out a good 100 yards or more, while on either side are lines of wilting red and yellow roses. The only thing that separates this garden and my targets next door is a small wooden panel fence. I creep towards the hurdle and peer over it, there's nobody about, perfect. In one smooth motion I hoist myself over the fence and land with a thud in the middle of a small flowering shrub.

The back of the house is just as impressive as the front. It had two huge bay windows on the first floor each with its own balcony, while directly in front of me is a patio area with two large floor-to-ceiling windows. Thick velvet curtains obscure the view inside. If this is Mr Stewart's house, he must be on one hell of a salary.

I creep towards the patio and gently place my ear to the glass. I hear nothing. I then spot a tiny crack where the two curtains don't quite join together. I crouch down and look through into what looks like a lounge, and right in the middle of the room I see them together.

The embrace that they are currently in shows me that they're much more than friends or colleagues. Their faces are locked together, his right hand on the back of her neck while his left is fumbling in his efforts to remove her tiny black dress. It's Paul Stewart all right.

I feel like a naughty schoolboy as I watch the action unfold slowly in front of me. The two lovers entwined in each other are totally oblivious to my unwelcome presence. I cannot pull myself away from the window as my breath steams the window. An overriding sense of jealousy fills my muddled head as I watch them go at it like prisoners finally released from a lengthy incarceration. I hear music blaring, obviously planned to set the mood; it stops me hearing the action. I feel confused about what's going on; in front of me is the guy I suspect of setting me up. How do I prove it? Why did he do it? These are the questions I need answering. I need to wait until he's alone and then I'll make my move.

I feel a blinding flash of pain as something lands violently across the back of my head. Dazed, I expertly role to one side, narrowly missing the second swing that lands with a soft thud on the concrete patio. I look up to see what appears to be a stocky built young man with white knuckles gripping the broken handle of a rake. It’s clear from his attire that he's the gardener, now turned vigilante. Lucky for me he's an amateur or I could be in some real trouble. Without giving the gardener a moment to strike again I use my right leg to kick his left ankle. The blow lands perfectly as I knock him off balance, giving me the chance to spring to my feet. There's still work to do as he's still clutching the rake, getting ready to swing again. I step close into him, my right hand flies out and quickly grasps the top of the rake in mid swing. I then smack my forehead into the bridge of his nose busting it open, ugly but effective. The move works perfectly as he releases his grip on his makeshift weapon and instinctively clutches his nose. Without giving him time to recover, I grab him in a tight neck lock and drag him away from the house towards the end of the garden, while cursing him for getting blood all over my arms.

We reach the top of the garden, and I pull him behind a small wooden shed, out of view of the house. I throw him to the ground, watching his attempt to stem the flow of blood cascading from his smashed nose with the left sleeve of his thick green woollen jumper. I try to ignore my pounding head as I feel a bump beginning to rise. I've had worse beatings.

I put my finger to my lips in a gesture of silence; the gardener gets the message. I keep one eye firmly on him while the other roams the ground, looking for something to keep him restrained. It's my lucky day, I think to myself, as I spot a ball of green gardening wire neatly stacked next to a collection of empty terracotta plant pots. That will do nicely. I pick up the wire and in an instant his hands and feet are bound together. "Sorry about this, I know you were only looking out for your boss," I quietly tell him.

"I'll make you a deal; you help me, I'll help you," I continue.

"What the hell do you want, Pervert?" he spits back at me.

"Look, Mate, it’s not what you think. Your boss and I have got issues that need resolving. I really need to get into that house; you must have a set of keys," I whisper. I reach down and start to frisk him.

"There in the right trouser pocket" he tells me. I reach into the pocket and pull out a small bunch of brass keys.

"Thanks for that. Now, I need one last favour, you keep quiet for a few minutes and I'll be back to untie you. Deal?" I ask.

"Do I have a choice?" He replies.

"No," I tell him as I creep off leaving the burly gardener struggling with the impossible task of removing the firm restraints.

I head back towards the house and take up my position. They’re still in the room but partially obscured by the sofa. There's no time like the present to make my move. Time is now against me, as I can’t trust the gardener to be quiet for long. I move to the side of the building where I find an old oak door that leads into the house, using the bunch of keys I carefully insert the first of six keys into the brass lock. It takes four attempts until I hear the sliding mechanism click into place. A gentle turn of the handle and the door creaks open.

The awful slow dance music that's still blaring out of the stereo hides my presence. Lucky for me they had it on or they could have heard the fracas outside. I step through a utility room full of white kitchen appliances into an L shaped kitchen, which has a door at the far end where the music is coming from. I stop in the kitchen and carefully open the first drawer I come to, lucky guess, I think to myself and I pull out a large carving knife. It’s time to get some answers.

The steel knife feels heavy in my hand as I approach the open archway leading to the lounge. To my horror, the music stops and an eerie silence envelops me. I quickly back-track through the kitchen to the utility room and wait. I try to control my breathing; it seems so loud, like a steam train in a tunnel. I don't want to give myself away.

"What do ya wanna drink, Baby?" Vicky’s familiar shrill voice calls out.

"Surprise me," A gruff voice replies. I look around the only place to hide is behind the open door that separates the two rooms. It’s like when I was a kid-playing hide and seek with my older brother. I always used to hide behind doors. I watch through the crack as she walks into the kitchen and retrieves two glasses from one of the cupboards. She then reaches for the scotch from a small collection of liquor bottles that lay on one corner of the kitchen worktop. It’s only then that my eyes drop down and I see Vicky in all her full glory; the elaborate black lace underwear leaves little to the imagination and I nearly forget the purpose of my little visit.

I continue to watch as she pours out two generous measures and then greedily take's a slug from the bottle before she replaces the cap and puts it aside. This girl's got a real thirst for booze. It's still early she either really likes a drink or needs it to sleep with Mr. Stewart. Either way she does not look happy from where I'm standing.

"Scotch good for you?" Vicky calls out.

"Sounds good honey but don't forget the ice," comes the reply.

"Sure thing." She shouts back.

Things are just about to get real complicated. I realise that my hiding place is just about to be compromised; I appear to be standing right next to the freezer. I have no time to move; Vicky is already heading this way with glass tumblers in her hands.

She walks into the room, I hear her put down the drinks and head towards me. To my surprise, she's oblivious to my presence. I watch her bend down beside me and slides open the freezer door, pulling out an ice cube tray. She then walks over to the drinks and with her back towards me, starts loading up the glasses with ice.

I won't have a better opportunity than this, so I make my move. In one fluid motion, I swing the door open and step forward. My left hand reaches for her hair and I pull it back, while my right hand reaches round and places the knife blade close to her throat.

"Not a word Vicky I don't want to hurt you" I whisper softly in her ear. "It's Richard, it's not you I'm after."

"How are those drinks coming?" I hear a voice call out.

"Baby you need to answer him or things will get real messy."

"I coming honey I just need the bathroom," she shouts.

"Good thinking girl," I congratulate her efforts to buy time.

"So what's your next move?" she asks me without a hint of fear.

"I don't know yet."

"Well, first of all, could you move the knife? You could hurt somebody with that," she casually asks. I consider my options and realise that we both know that I'm not going to hurt her. I withdraw the knife from her neck and step back. "That's better" she replies. My eyes again are drawn to her fine physique. Inappropriate I know, but I can't help myself. "There's plenty of time for that later," she acknowledges my gaze with a knowing stare.

"But right now you need to get the hell out of here or you're going to ruin the whole investigation," she tells me.

"Investigation?" I ask.

"I'll tell you later, no time now. I'll meet you back at my house, but please get the hell out of here," she whispers.

"Where are those drinks baby? I'm getting thirsty in here." The voice from the lounge calls out.

"Coming," Vicky replies. With that, she picks up the drinks. Giving me a wink, she heads off towards the lounge, while I stand dumbstruck with a useless knife in my hand, all the while watching her firm sexy body wiggling back to the lounge.

Seven

I stand there completely dumbstruck, no idea of my next move. I don't know whom to trust anymore. It seems that the years of gut instinct and hunches are no help to me now. Who is this girl? Who does she work for? It does make some kind of sense, I suppose, all her creeping around after dark. The fact that she never ratted me to the police works in her favour. Even so I've got to tread carefully.

The noise of the two lovebirds in the other room is clearly audible above the constant drone of the electro music blaring out of the speakers. They were clearly not that thirsty after all. Well as they're both busy, I'm sure that they won't mind me having a little look around the place.

I wait patiently for a few more minutes, until I'm sure that they're both in that special place. The loud groans, moans and shrieks confirm they're oblivious to the outside world. I walk softly through the kitchen and creep into the lounge, the scene of all the animalistic noises. I try to ignore the sweaty nakedness happening on the sofa, walking straight to the open door on the other side of the room and into the hallway.

There is a spiral staircase that sits proudly in the centre of this large open-air room, with several other doors leading off in different directions, but a quick peek does not reveal anything of interest, a dining room, a storage room and a make-shift gym. I take the stairs that spiral up to the first floor and out into a large mezzanine.

It takes me a few seconds to find the bedroom; the garish purple and orange of the painted walls makes my teeth hurt. The first thing I notice is the picture that hangs proudly in the centre of the wall directly opposite the enormous king sized bed. It's a blown up family photo with what looks like Mr Stewart's wife and two teenage kids. "Bingo," I mutter to myself, so the guys married. The perfect husband! He doesn't sound too perfect at the moment.

The bedroom has two doors leading off of it; one is to an en-suite bathroom, while the other is firmly locked. This immediately peaks my interest. Who locks rooms in their own house? I need to get in there. There are two ways to get into the room, the first being to creep around the house until I find the keys, which are probably in Mr. Stewarts trouser pockets. I decide to take the second option and give the door a good kicking. It takes a few attempts for the door to splinter open. The music downstairs tells me they're still too wrapped up in each other to notice the noise.

The broken door opens to reveal what appears to be Mr. Stewart's study. It's a small boxy room with two light grey metal filing cabinets sitting beside an old antique looking mahogany bureau. The bureau is locked and the key is nowhere to be seen. Whatever is in there, he clearly does not want anybody to see it. Now my curiosity is really aroused. It feels a shame to have to break open such a nice piece of furniture. I pick up a letter opener and use it to wedge open the door. It just takes a little downwards pressure for the lock to pop and the door flings open.

There in front of me I see two large brown envelopes both "stamped private and confidential". I open one up and peer inside. It's full of photographs, dirty photographs not the kind of thing that you would find in a family album. It's then that I notice who the people in the photo are. It's Mr Stewart and Jess together in a series of sexual clinches. It appears that they took the photos themselves; it’s pure filth. I cannot bear to look at them, seeing another man paw at her like that. I pick up both envelopes fold them and stuff them into my back pocket. It's then that I hear the commotion downstairs.

I run to the bedroom window and look out towards the garden. Then I see the police speaking to the dishevelled gardener. Things are about to get very tricky.

Eight

The policeman in the garden has a quizzical look on his face as the gardener recounts his story. It's then that I see Mr Stewart in an awful purple dressing gown making his way into the garden to find out what the commotion is all about. I continue to watch as another two uniformed cops enter the garden and join Mr. Stewart in conversation. I just hope that they think I'm a burglar or a sex pest or the cops will be everywhere. I've got to get out of this house quick smart or it's all over.

I head towards the staircase and look down for signs of life. It appears that everybody's outside listening to the gardener's story. So I make my way downstairs and into the large hallway and run straight into a hot and flustered Vicky who is still in a state of partial dress.

"We must stop meeting like this" I quip.

"They're heading this way, use the front door," Vicky rushes to tell me. Panic spreads across my body as I realise the predicament that I'm in. "Run you fool," she urges me. I hear voices approaching and finally run to the front door and pull open the handle. It's locked. Shit. The voices are getting louder so I open the first door I come to and rush in, shutting it quietly behind me.

The room is a spacious dining area with a large oval table occupying the centre and a selection of dark wooden chairs neatly surrounding it. On closer inspection I notice that there's only one door in and out. So I'm stuck in here with nowhere to go.

I look to the windows that are hidden behind thick velvet curtains. If I was twenty years younger and ten pounds lighter I might have been able to wriggle through but I'm not going to attempt it. I'd rather be caught than lose my dignity from being stuck in a window.

It's then that I hear footsteps and then voices in the hallway. "What's going on?" I hear Vicky's shrill little voice coyly ask.

"It appears we have an intruder in the house and these gentleman want to have a look around," Mr Stewart replies, obviously annoyed due to the interruption of his morning’s sexual workout.

"That's funny as I just heard a noise from upstairs and was about to go and investigate," Vicky coolly lies. I imagine that she's using those sweet Bambi eyes for all they’re worth.

"Leave it to us, Madam," a gruff male voice answers.

The sound of footsteps heading upstairs relaxes me slightly. Good girl, Vicky. I press my eye towards the keyhole to spy an empty hallway; it's now or never. I open the door and purposefully march through the hall to the kitchen and out towards the back door. I reach the back of the house in seconds and step out into the cool breeze of morning.

There in front of me on the concrete patio I see the gardener still holding a handkerchief against his nose. It's clear from his expression that I'm the last person that he wants to see. I head towards him. Just as he is about to call out, I stop him with a well-positioned fist in his mouth. I watch as he collapses to the ground like an abused mannequin. I step over his body and head towards the fence and jump it in once smooth fluid motion, landing softly on the other side.

"Stop, this is the police," I hear a stern voice call out behind me.

"Shit, Shit, Shit!" I pick up speed and hightail it out of there. I turn my head for a second to see the police clambering over the fence behind me. The chase is on.

I sprint back through the neighbour's beautifully manicured garden past the gate and out into the street. I look back; the police are in hot pursuit. There's no time to catch my breath I run out into the street and towards the parked car. Strangely, the only thought going through my head as I run is the sight of Vicky in her underwear holding two tumblers of whisky. The problem being, as I'm a dry alcoholic, I'm not sure if it's the girl or the drink that I long for.

Muscles like pistons pumping, sinews stretching, sweat pouring, cherry blossom trees whipping past, and I continue to run. The lampposts become obstacles as I bob and weave past them. The police continue to chase. There's no point heading for the car, no time to hotwire it, I'd be caught in seconds. No choice but to keep running. I'll tire out these overweight beat cops, just got to keep running.

My sore feet pound the asphalt. The brown leather shoes I'm wearing are no use for the punishment they are about to receive. The quiet suburb streets are now alive with the sound of shouting policemen. I'm too busy to listen to their demands; they may scream and shout, but I'm not stopping - not now. Not after all I've been through. The curtains must be twitching all over the neighbourhood; no doubt I'll be the talk of the town at the next neighbourhood watch meeting.

The end of the road is in sight as I pass by the stolen car I used to get me into this predicament. I twist my neck to see the police still chasing. How long can I keep this up? Looks like my shoes will disintegrate before these determined coppers would cease the chase. The quaint little road I'm currently running through hits a T-junction up ahead and onto a main highway. It'll be easier to shake them off if I head for the traffic.

I've got to be brave, no choice but head down and go for it. I'm running out of pavement. The cars are screaming from right to left. I see an opening and charge across the road towards the grass verge that separates this busy road. The cars hit the brakes, tooting their horns as I kamikaze across. The verge looks like a paradise island as I race for the prize, ignoring the high-speed danger all around me.

My eyes sting with the sweat of the chase as I finally reach safety in the middle of the street. The cops have stopped to wait for the heavy traffic to slow down before they make their move. There's no time to waste as I leap over the metal barrier that divides the road and prepare myself to run the gauntlet one last time. Three deep breaths and off I go. I sprint across the last section of road, blind to the oncoming danger. I just hope the drivers are paying attention or I'm history.

I greet the pavement like a long lost friend as I make it across, leaving the coppers struggling for breath on the other side. That was a real close shave. I reach round and gently pat my pockets; the photos are still there.

I need to get off the street; I'm like a sitting duck out here. I need to find some cover. I've no choice but to head to Vicky's place and think things through. I feel done in. My age is beginning to show; too much liquor and too many smokes have damaged my body. That was too close. I need to sleep. I cannot keep going like this.

It takes a moment for me to get my breath back and for the burning in my lungs to subside before I can continue to run. I need to get back to the city and away from this hellish suburb. I continue to run for what feels like an age before I spot an underground entrance to a dilapidated subway station. It's only then that I spot a squad car hurtling towards me. Do these guys ever give up?

There's no where else to run so I head for the stairs that lead downwards into a poorly lit deserted station. My eyes dart to and fro like a caged animal looking for an exit. I then spot a sign for the platform to get me back towards the relative safety of the city.

The hard-edged footsteps that follow remind me that I'm not out of the woods yet. I follow the underground assault course of barriers and stairs that finally leads me to a desolate and poorly lit underground platform.

It must be my lucky day, I note, as a city bound train glides its way towards me. It’s time to lose the boys in blue who are still dedicatedly following me. Lucky for me, they’re just out of sight. I turn right and sprint down to the end of the platform and towards the oncoming train. The graffiti tagged silver train speeds past me and the driver starts to apply the brakes.

Once the train passes me I leap awkwardly onto the tracks and run into the tunnel and away from the now stationary train as fast as my ageing legs can carry me. Once I'm a fair distance away, I turn around just in time to see the chasing police board the waiting train. Fools. It's now time to get myself back to Vicky's place and figure this thing out. I'm too tired to run anymore; I need this to end one way or another.

I need to rest for a while and make sure I've lost the cops. My eyes sting from sleep deprivation. The worlds getting dizzy. I feel woozy, like a novice drinker. I need sleep to put the world back on an even keel. I can't live like this anymore.

It's funny really, all those years chasing criminals and now I'm on the receiving end. I never thought that I would wind up here, on the run, wanted by the law. I just want to scream, let out all the anger and frustration I'm feeling. I'm losing control.

I take a seat on the back of the track and wait for the aching in my legs to subside. There's no chance of sleeping here as the peace is shattered every couple of minutes by passing trains. I just want to lie down and forget the world here in this dank, dark tunnel.

I strain in the darkness to see the time on my cheap watch and realise I've been sitting here by the tracks for over an hour. Strange, it felt like minutes. It's time to move again. I get up dust myself off and head back towards the station. I stroll back onto the platform and plonk my sorry ass on a bench and wait impatiently for the next train to arrive.

I'm not sitting long before another graffiti-covered train rolls into the station. I board an empty carriage and take a seat. Within minutes the train doors close and it pulls out of the station.

The journey towards the big smoke feels like a dream, the scenery flies past me from right to left. The greens of the suburbs soon turn to grey as the city’s outskirts whizz by in a blur of colour before my red bloodshot eyes. The fat old sun is low in the sky and the city is alive with colour, I'll be there soon.

The train finally pulls into the city's central station and the doors automatically open. "All change," comes the muffled voiced over the trains decrepit speaker system. I've got to be careful. This station is one of the most policed areas of the city. I need to keep my head down and get out of here swiftly. I leave the train and head straight for the exit, careful not to look anybody in the eye.

I'm back on familiar streets breathing in the putrid air of this dirty old town. It ain't much, but it’s home. I exit the station, preparing myself for the long walk to Vicky's place, I briefly think about hotwiring another car, but my conscience gets the better of me. I might be a wanted man, but I want to stay on the right path.

The evening walk towards Vicky's is a struggle. Just putting one foot in front of the other is a real chore, I could have used the underground subway, but the risk of capture is too high. I want to get to the house and take a good look at the photos and figure this whole sorry mess out. I know Vicky's up to her eyeballs in it. One way or another, it all ends tomorrow. I just can't keep going anymore.

I zombie my way through the underbelly of this great city oblivious to the people around me. My exhausted confused thoughts are whirling through my tired mind like laundry in a broken tumble dryer. I can barely see in front of my face and yet somehow, I manage to navigate the mean streets that snake across the city like an unsolvable maze. The only thing keeping me going is a need for the truth, my fate is secondary, I don't care anymore. I just want it all to stop.

I'm not sure how long I've been on the road, but at last I enter familiar surroundings. There in front of me is the house I've been aiming for - 182 Weak Street. There's no point trying to break in, after all she knows I'm coming. The house is well lit, so someone's clearly home. I'm just hoping she hasn't set me up, but it's too late to turn back now. And, after all, I've got nowhere else to go.

I stride purposefully up to the heavy wooden door, bang loudly on it, take a few paces back and wait. The door opens quickly and there in front of me stands Vicky. It looks like she's just stepped out of the shower. Her hair glows from just being washed and the smell of eucalyptus fills the night air. She's clearly comfortable around me, as she is wearing light grey sweat pants and a pristine white tee shirt. Even when she's not dressed up, this girl's got it in spades.

"What took you so long?" she quizzes.

"It's a long walk back," I reply sarcastically.

"You coming in then?" her shrill little voice asks. With that she turns round and walks into the house, leaving the door open for me to follow.

"Here goes nothing," I whisper to myself. It's now time to find out which side this girl is on. I step through the threshold and quietly close the door behind me.

"I'm in here," comes Vicky's voice from the kitchen. I follow the sound of her voice and find her filling up a tumbler with scotch. She turns to face me and points the bottle towards me like a loaded gun, "Want one?" she asks.

The temptation is nearly too much to bear. I look down and stare at the already poured glass, and for a moment get lost in the glowing amber liquid. I pick the glass up and bring it expertly to my nose, like a seasoned wine taster. I inhale the sweet smell of the fine malt whisky, remembering. One won't hurt, I tell myself, after the day I've had, I deserve a drink. It might help calm my nerves, after all. Who's to know? I finally snap out of it and put down the glass.

"No thanks honey, a glass of water will be fine," I coolly tell her. Years of AA have finally paid off as the temptation fades into the background. My attention turns away from the scotch and back to the beauty standing before me.

"So how was your day honey?" I ask as Vicky hands me a glass of ice-cold water.

"Not bad, you?" Vicky replies playing along.

"So-so," I confirm.

"Shall we take this to the lounge?" Vicky asks.

"After you," I tell her.

I watch as Vicky brushes past me and heads for the lounge. My eyes are drawn instinctively towards her fine body as she wiggles her way past me. I'm sure she does it on purpose, especially now that my defences are down. I instinctively follow her into the lounge and plonk myself on the cream leather sofa opposite her.

"I hope you don't mind but these gentleman would like to ask you a few questions," Vicky tells me. It's then that I notice the three smartly dressed men standing silently in the corner of the room.

Nine

"Good evening Richard, I'm Detective Inspector Stubbs. I've been looking forward to meeting you." The middle of the three tells me. He then reaches inside his suit jacket and pulls out some ID to confirm his identity. My eyes dart to the door but common sense soon kicks in. I've got no energy left to run. Where am I going to run to? I'm done running. There's only one option left for me and that's to hope justice prevails. Who knows? These guys could be here to help.

"Nice to meet you Inspector, how can I be of assistance"? I casually ask the rotund policeman.

"Well I believe you're currently in a spot of bother, and we might be able to help you out," Inspector Stubbs replies.

"Help me out? How do you plan to do that? Last time I checked I was a wanted felon, with my face splashed all over the papers. How are you possibly going to make that all disappear?" I enquire sarcastically as I sink into the sofa, on a quest for comfort.

"It's not you we're after Richard, we believe that you were an unfortunate little pawn in a much bigger picture. It's Paul Stewart we're after," Stubbs' hoarse voice explains.

"Well what are you waiting for? There's the door, I can even give you his house address if you want. So what do you need me for?" I ask, unable to understand what the hell's going on. My head's spinning from all of this. Things just keep spiralling out of control.

"That's the problem, Richard. You may have already noticed that he controls most of the cops in this town. We need direct evidence to nail the son of a bitch to the wall for what he's done." The inspector starts to pace the room. "There's only a few of us who know the truth, but we're not able to use the Force's resources to bring him down. That's where your special talents come in," Stubbs continues.

"Sorry inspector, you've lost me completely. All I know is that he is, sorry was, my boss and I believe that he's somehow responsible for murdering Jessica and pinning the blame on me. In the last few days all I've managed to find out is that he was sleeping with her at one point and that he enjoyed taking photos of his steamy encounters." I pause for a second to compose myself. My eyes flit towards Vicky and rest on her warm face. She turns to meet my gaze and gives me a reassuring smile.

I fight back the tears of grief. In my current state, there is no use in even trying to keep my emotions at bay. I want to let out the hurt I'm feeling for the loss of Jess, as well as for myself. I don't know who I am anymore. I just want to sleep.

"Richard we really don't have the time for full details but I'll try and fill you in as much as I can. Stewart as you know left the Force to set up the agency, but it's still attached to the service and with government backing. The idea was to use methods that the police, by law, are not allowed to nail perps. You know the score, break the law to enforce the law. The problem started when Mr Stewart realised that no one was policing him. He now believes he's above the law and has started to use his team for his own purposes. The man's into fraud, vice and protection rackets - the whole works and it's all funded with government money, resources and a team of crack agents who have no idea whose side they're on." Stubbs pauses to pull out a packet of cigarettes from his jacket pocket and sparks one up.

"So where do I fit in?" I inquire, unable to comprehend my role in all of this.

Vicky now stands up and carries on where the inspector left off. "Well Rich, from what I can gather, your ex Jess was not as innocent as you believed. We have evidence that she was blackmailing Stewart by threatening to send pictures of their intimate moments together to his wife. So he put a stop to it, and unfortunately you got used as the scapegoat due to your past connection with her."

"All this over sex?" I struggle to announce. It has all been about not letting the wife know what he was up to. Bastard. "Vicky I better have that drink now," I calmly ask her.

"Richard I know this is all coming as a shock but we need your help to put him away," Stubbs finally asks.

"I'll do what ever it takes to bring him down." I reach for the full tumbler of Scotch Vicky is holding out to me.

The scotch burns the back of my throat as I swig it down in one. I then sink back into the sofa and let the fiery liquid do its magic. I close my eyes and savour the taste whilst trying to block out the others in the room. God, that feels good. It's been so long, my old friend, nice to have you back. "Any chance of a refill?" I inquire.

"Later Richard," Vicky hits back.

"So what do you want me to do?" I ask wearily.

"We need you to wear a wire and pay a visit to Mr Stewart and see if you can get a confession," Stubbs' gruff voice asks.

"Sure thing boss," I reply. I then reach into my pocket and retrieve the role of film and the photos I snatched earlier. "This might come in handy." I casually toss them towards Inspector Stubbs before standing. "Well if you gentleman could excuse me I'm done for the evening, I'm sure Vicky will fill me in tomorrow," I explain before making my way upstairs on the hunt for a bed. I head straight for Vicky's bedroom and collapse onto the bed and within seconds I'm out for the count.

My eyes open slowly and I'm momentarily blinded, as the morning sun is sneaking through the closed curtains. I then turn round to see Vicky's smiling face staring back at me. "Morning sleepy head," her shrill little voice announces.

“Morning honey, I always knew we would end up in bed together," I reply. Vicky lets out a coy smile and leans over to kiss me. The rest of the morning is a blur of bedroom activity.

Morning fades into the afternoon, and finally we both leave the bedroom to prepare for the day ahead. It takes minutes for me to shower and shave, and by early afternoon, I'm sitting comfortably on the sofa waiting for Vicky to fill me in on what to do next.

"My, you scrub up nice, I was wondering what lay behind that beard of yours," Vicky compliments.

"Thanks honey, so what's the plan?" I ask impatiently.

“Well that's all down to you Richard. I'll supply the wire and you tell me how you want to approach it." she replies.

"You’re close with him right?" I ask jealously.

"You know I am Rich," comes her cat like reply.

"Well, why don't you arrange another little meeting with our man in a nice little secluded location and let me do the rest?"

"Sounds good," she tells me.

I barely hear Vicky as she whispers something into the phone. I look around and my eyes rest on the half empty bottle of scotch sitting proudly on a small table under the window. One won't hurt. I stand up and make my way over to the bottle of joy.

“Thirsty Richard? How about a nice cup of coffee?" Vicky asks as she walks briskly into the room and picks up the bottle before I can get to it.

"Ok, Honey."

"He's coming round tonight Rich so you better be ready," she tells me.

"Oh, I'll be ready all right, just get me the wire and get the hell out of here," I coolly reply.

The afternoon soon fades into evening while I sit and wait for Mr Stewart's arrival. The wire is firmly in place and Vicky is upstairs hiding. It won't be long now and all this will finally be over. I glance at my cheap airport watch. Nine p.m. He should be here soon. I reach over to the tumbler and drain the last of the scotch from the glass. I soon feel the heat of the liquor sending waves of relaxation throughout my body. I take one last drag on the cigarette that's been smouldering away, neglected in the ashtray, and inhale deeply.

I clutch the kitchen knife white-knuckle tight in my right hand and wait. My right leg twitches uncontrollably as I sit impatiently for him to arrive. It's then that I hear a soft knock.

"It's open," comes Vicky's shrill little voice from upstairs. I rise to my feet in an instant, head over to the lounge door and hide behind it. I hear the front door open slowly and someone enter the house.

"I'll be down in a second, make yourself at home," Vicky calls out.

“Don't get dressed on my account," Stewart’s sleazy voice replies.

The sound of the front door closing tells me it's nearly time as I try to control my erratic breathing. Through the crack in the door I watch him slowly make his way into the room and head toward the sofa. He has no time to sit as I'm onto him in an instant teeth bared and knife in hand. Surprise is my ally as I grab his slicked back greasy hair and yank him towards me.

"I wouldn't move if I were you," I warn him.

"What the fu!!" Is all I can make out as I slowly squeeze his jewels.

"Did I ask you to talk?" Stewart buckles to the floor but the knife at his neck soon straightens him up. I bet Inspector Stubbs was not intending for the chat to go like this. Who cares? This bastard deserves everything he gets. I then give him another fresh squeeze. That's got to hurt, I think to myself.

"Me and you need to talk," I tell him

"I'll do what ever you want," comes the feeble reply of a man whose balls are in danger.

"It's Richard, remember me? Why did you do it?" I ask purposefully.

"The bitch was blackmailing me; she wanted a slice of the action, too bloody greedy for her own good."

"Why get me involved?" I shout in his ear as my anger rises.

"She told me you supplied the pictures, that you were in it together," Stewart sobs as he feels my vice like grip tighten around his nuts.

"What pictures?" I quiz.

"Of us together. She told me that you had them and if anything happened to her you would send them to the wife and the papers." It's pathetic - a simple squeeze and this guy is singing like a canary.

"So you never had any photos of us?" He asks as tears of pain run down his fat sweaty cheeks.

"No, wrong guy, chief. I don't have anything anymore the police have got it all," is my smug reply.

It is then that I notice a wry smile come over his face like a cat that got the cream. "If I were you, I'd put the knife down," he calmly tells me. I notice Vicky at the door with a gun in her hand.

"Drop the knife, Richard," Vicky tells me.

I stand there dumfounded, unable to comprehend the situation. "What the hell is going on here?" I ask.

"Drop it," comes her cold reply.

The knife slips out of my hand and lands on the floor with a dull thud. Stewart breaks from my grip and hobbles over to the sofa to rest his aching balls.

"Thanks Richard," Stewart's gruff voice tells me.

"What for?" I ignorantly inquire.

"We just needed to know if you had any evidence left against me, although it appears that you were stupid enough to hand it all over last night. Obviously, I didn’t train you well enough." Stewart had a sly smile on his face.

My eyes focus on Vicky's stern face while her Bambi eyes stare right back at me. I've been set up, fooled. I knew she wasn't to be trusted. All the years of training and I'm outsmarted by a dame. Damn she was good, had me fooled. She'll really go far, this one.

I watch as she turns to face Stewart. "How’d I do?" she asks in that shrill voice.

"Just great, Baby."

The gunshot makes me jump backwards in a futile attempt to find safety. It is then I realize that the shot was not meant for me. Stewart's body lies twitching on the floor. A single bullet hole in the centre of his forehead tells me it is the end of the line for Mr. Paul Stewart.

"What now?" I calmly ask.

"You can join Jess now Rich."

A loud explosion is the last thing I hear, and then the world goes black.

The End

For Now

www.ingramcontent.com/pod-product-compliance
Ingram Content Group UK Ltd.
Pitfield, Milton Keynes, MK11 3LW, UK
UKHW041921190726
13854UKWH00003B/1361